Rise and Shine!

By Constance Allen
Cover Illustrated by Joe Ewers
Illustrated by David Prebenna

Published by Bendon, Ashland, OH 44805
bendonpub.com
1-888-5-BENDON

Printed in China
82007-TG F 0514

Rise and shine! The sun is coming up! On Sesame Street, little monsters and birds and grouches are still snug in their beds.

Barkley is ready for an early morning walk.
The baker is baking cookies and cakes and bread.
Up and at 'em, everyone—or there won't be any left!

In the country, Farmer Grover gets ready to milk the cows. "Rise and shine, little cows!" he calls.

Time to get up,
Mommy and Daddy!
Baby Natasha is
ready to play!

Ernie wakes up
his buddy Bert.
"Rise and shine,
Bert! The sun is
coming up!"

In the city, Oscar wakes up to watch the trash collectors. "Bang those cans!" he yells. "That's it, boys! Crash 'em! Clank 'em! Heh-heh-heh."

The Count is up early, delivering newspapers.
"One newspaper! Two newspapers! Three newspapers!"
he counts. "Rise and shine, everyone!
It's a marvelous day for counting!"

Herry Monster huffs and puffs on his morning jog.

Big Bird splashes in his morning bath with some friends.
"La! La! La! La! La!" he sings as he scrubs.

Don't forget to
brush your fangs!

Be sure to comb
your head—and face
and elbows and knees!

"What should I wear today?" Bert wonders.

Rise and shine! Breakfast is served at Hooper's Store!

It's a beautiful sunny day on Sesame Street!
All the monsters and birds and grouches
have come out to play.

Rise and shine, little Elmo!